# Subway Ride

Heather Lynn Miller • Illustrated by Sue Ramá

Charlesbridge

To Lola, who set me on the right track
—H. L. M.

To Dr. Steven Shichman, with my gratitude
—S. R.

The illustration for the Moscow subway station was based on
a photograph by Bee Flowers, which was adapted with permission.

Published by Charlesbridge
85 Main Street
Watertown, MA 02472
(617) 926-0329
www.charlesbridge.com

**Library of Congress Cataloging-in-Publication Data**
Miller, Heather Lynn.
    Subway ride / Heather Lynn Miller ; illustrated by Sue Ramá.
        p. cm.
    ISBN 978-1-58089-111-0 (reinforced for library use)
    1. Subways—Juvenile literature. I. Ramá, Sue. II. Title.
TF845.M55 2008
388.4'28—dc22                    2008007249

Printed in China
(hc) 10 9 8 7 6 5 4 3 2 1

Illustrations done as a digital collage of watercolor art
Display type and text type set in Mister Earl and Ogre
Title type hand-lettered by Sue Ramá
Color separations by Chroma Graphics, Singapore
Printed and bound by Everbest Printing Company, Ltd.,
    through Four Colour Imports Ltd., Louisville, Kentucky
Production supervision by Brian G. Walker
Designed by Diane M. Earley and Sue Ramá

Down,
down,
down.

Step down below
to see the world.

Now off we go!

We pay our fare.
We turn the gate.

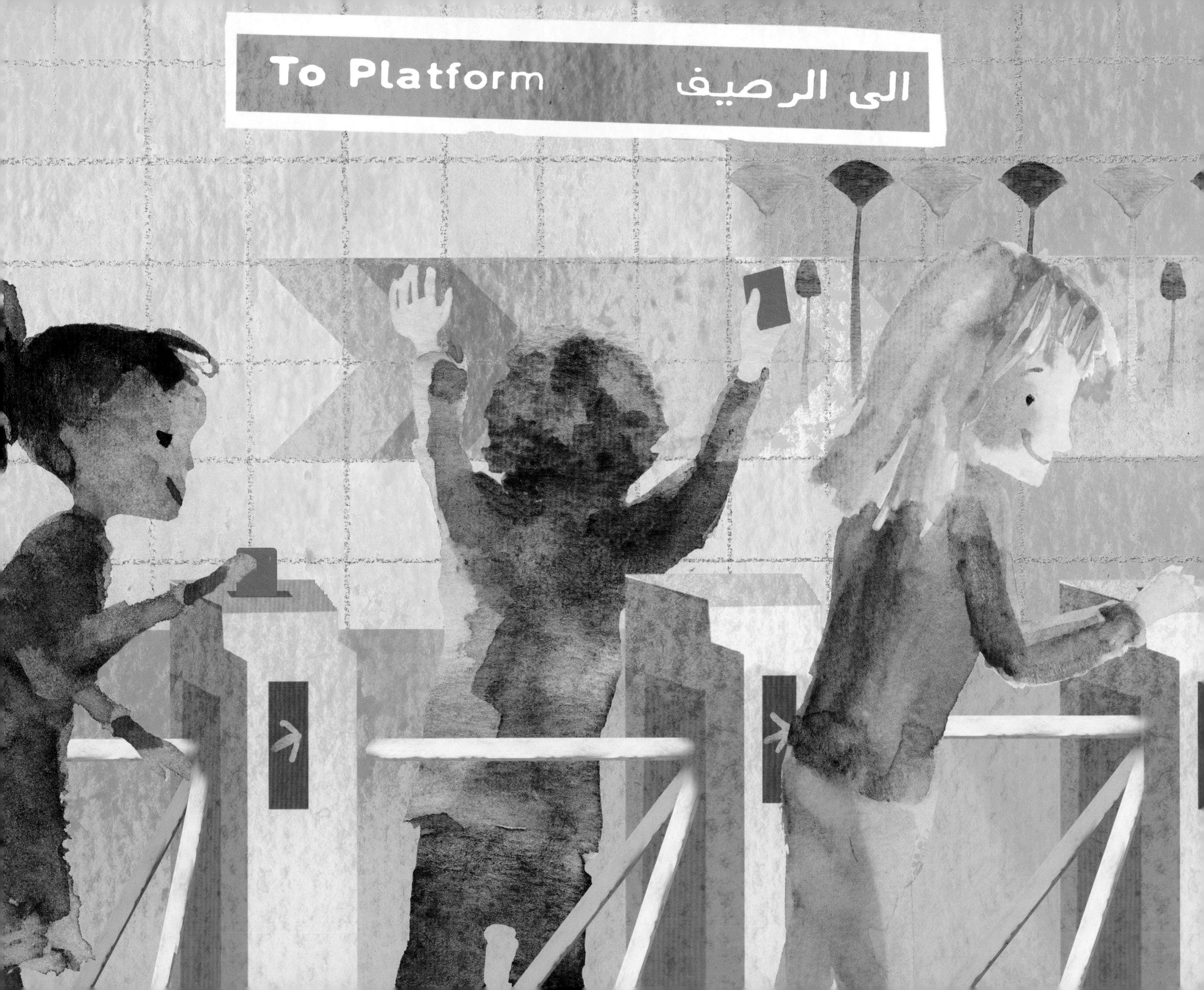
To Platform
الى الرصيف

Moscow
Mockbá

Underground we
wait . . .
wait . . .
wait . . .

Saxophone blasts
jazzy vibes.

Drums and cymbals
jam and jive.

Rumbling, roaring—
blurring speed.

Silver bullet.
Rushing breeze.

We step on quickly.
Move aside.

Doors slide shut.
Our turn to ride!

Busy folks
step off and on.
We stay put.
Our trip is long.

Washington, DC

Doors slide open.
We slide back.

Subway whizzes down the track.

We bump and sway.
We hold on tight.
We zip through tunnels
dark as night.

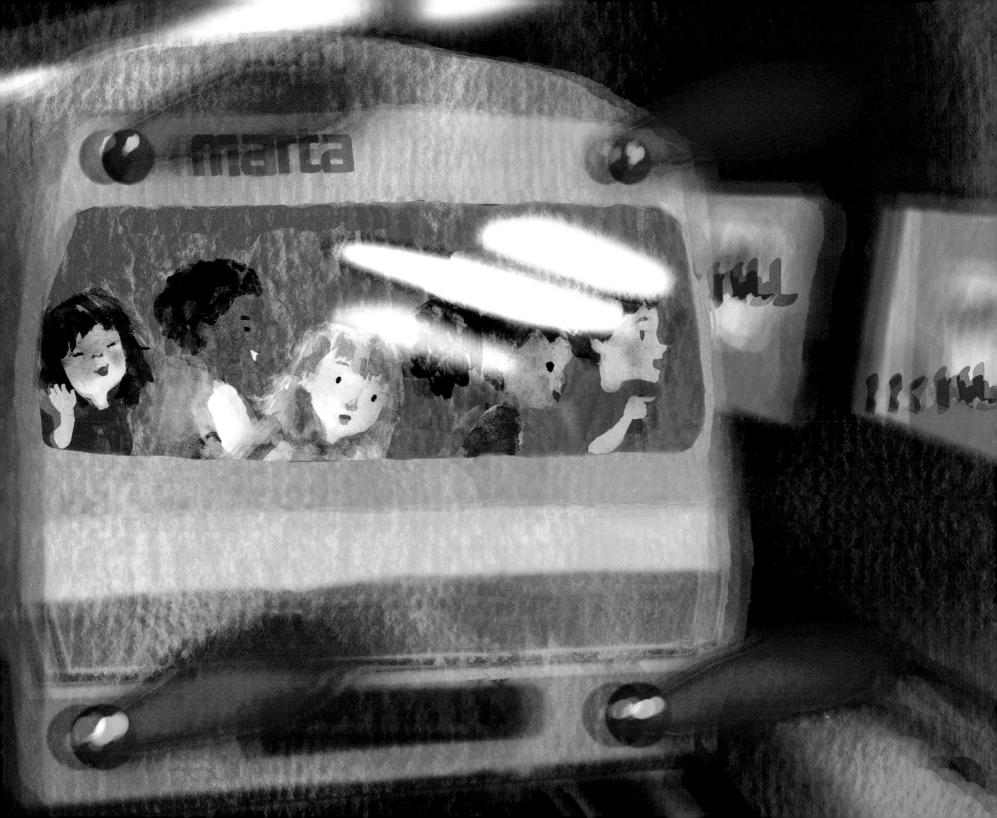

Mexico City
Ciudad de México

Clomping, stomping,
shuffling feet
step to the clacking
subway beat.

"Last stop!" we hear
the driver shout.

Doors open wide.
We step out.

Step up,
step up,
from the dark—

a celebration in the park!

All over the world, subways snake through tunnels deep below city streets. Listed here are just some of the cities that depend on underground trains to move millions of people from place to place. If you've never traveled on a subway, chances are you will someday. Whether you take a trip on the Tube in London or ride the T-Bana in Stockholm, you are sure to have an exciting ride!

## Atlanta

Atlanta's MARTA (Metropolitan Atlanta Rapid Transit Authority) was the first subway to try a new type of advertising. In September 2001, a long row of lighted signs was set up inside a subway tunnel. As the train whizzed past, riders saw a twenty-second animated commercial in what was normally a dark, empty tunnel.

## Cairo

Cairo, Egypt, has the only subway in Africa. With over 22 million people traveling above ground, Cairo needed an underground train. The first line opened in 1987. Only women are allowed in the first car of the subway. A ticket for the Cairo Metro is inexpensive, costing one Egyptian pound, or about twenty cents.

## Chicago

Most of Chicago's trains travel on elevated tracks, so the system is called the "L." Only two lines run underground. The soil under the city is very wet and sticky. Tunnel builders had to take special care to prevent cave-ins while they cut through the slippery clay.

## London

On January 10, 1863, a three-mile stretch of subway track was put into service in London, England. This was the first subway system in the world. Riders on the Tube pay particular attention to proper behavior. They are expected to give up their seats to those in need, step aside to let others pass, and refrain from eating stinky foods.

## Mexico City

On September 4, 1969, the first section of Mexico City's subway system opened. Construction on the Metro has never stopped, and today over 175 stations serve the city. Some Metro stations are decorated with murals by well-known Mexican artists, while others contain unique artifacts. The Pino Suárez station contains remnants of an Aztec temple that were found during construction.

## Moscow

Moscow's Metro stations are so beautiful that they are called "the people's palaces." The stations are decorated with stained glass, mosaics, and lavish paintings. This fantastic world of elegance and beauty has been used for more than just transportation. During World War II the Metro stations were used as shelters to help keep people safe while the city above was being attacked.

# New York City

New York's subway system has 468 stations—more than any other subway in the world. Before the creation of its modern electric subway, New York had other types of trains traveling beneath it. The city's first underground train ran under Broadway and was powered by the pressure created by a giant fan.

# Stockholm

In Stockholm the subway system is called the Tunnelbana, or T-Bana. The surfaces of the T-Bana's walls and ceilings are irregular, making travelers feel as if they are exploring a cave. Some walls have been painted with spectacular murals, while other areas showcase sculptures, mosaics, and other artistic displays.

# Tokyo

The subway cars in Tokyo are clean, quick, and crowded. Sometimes the trains are so packed with people that passengers don't even need to hang onto the handrails. They just lean on one another in the cramped cars. Many children take the subway to school every day.

# Washington, DC

The Metro in Washington, DC, is known for being clean and fast. The system's trains can travel at 85 miles per hour over 103 miles of track, from the suburbs of Maryland and Virginia to the heart of the capital city. The longest escalator in the Western hemisphere is located at the Wheaton station. It climbs over 230 feet from the tracks to the street.